A PROMISE IS FOREVER

A Promise is Forever

A WORLD WAR II STORY

Donald F. Hrinya

Meraki Press

Contents

Paperback ISBN: 979-8-9873516-2-8

Cover Design and Layout: Katie Zeliger
Editing: Christie Beckwith
Formatting: Wyeth Doty

Printed in the United States of America
Meraki Press LLC
www.merakipress.org

First Publishing in 2019.
Second Edition, May 2023

This book is dedicated to all who served in World War II in defense of freedom.

1

Beechtree Memorial Cemetery

Brockway, PA 2000

Jimmer had no way of knowing that a chance meeting in the summer of 2000 would change his life forever. He had just pulled up to the Beechtree Memorial Cemetery in Brockway, Pennsylvania, where he saw an older man fall to his knees weeping a few rows away. After parking, Jimmer approached the man and asked, "Are you alright, sir?"

The older man gained his composure as he lifted himself off the ground. "Look at me weeping like a baby. It's been so long since I visited him that my emotions got to me." Jimmer glanced at the writing on the tombstone before them:

Ed Hrinya 1914-1995 WWII Veteran

The older man introduced himself as Tom Smith, "but everybody calls me Smitty."

Jim replied, "Nice to meet you, Smitty. Everybody calls me Jimmer."

"Jimmer, are you from this area? Did you happen to know Ed?"

"Yes, I did, Smitty."

Smitty continued, "I knew him in the war. Did he ever tell you about the war?"

"No, he didn't," Jimmer replied.

"So, I guess you didn't know he was a hero."

"A hero, Smitty?"

"Isn't that what you call someone who saves your life?"

"He saved your life, huh?"

"Mine and five or six other men I knew, and he indirectly saved countless others."

"I wonder why he never said anything?"

Smitty answered, "It may be because of a promise he made to his mother."

"What promise, Smitty?"

"Jimmer, if you're not in a hurry, how would you like to hear about Ed?" Jimmer told Smitty he had some time and would like that very much.

"I'll tell you about him if you promise to do me a favor when I finish," Smitty said.

Jimmer agreed.

Smitty began, "I first met Ed in the spring of 1944 in

England. We were there preparing for Operation Overlord. Do you know what that was, Jimmer?"

"Yes, the D-Day landing," Jimmer replied.

"That's right. Shortly after arriving, I asked the men there if I had the correct barracks - umm, barracks 16, I believe it was."

Ed was the first to speak up, "That's what it says on the door." he retorted. Then asked, "Who are you guys?"

"I'm Tom Smith, but everyone calls me Smitty. The man behind me here is John Lee."

"My name is Ed Hrinya. That soldier over there is Kenneth Tuck. We call him Tucky." I suppose many of us were arriving from the same part of the states because Ed asked us, "Are either of you two from Pennsylvania?" I told him I was from Gettysburg.

Tucky said, "Tell him where you're from, Ed."

Ed said, "Brockway. Y'ever heard of it?" I told him that I hadn't.

Tucky said, "See, Ed, no one has heard of it. Are you sure it exists?"

Ed said, "It exists. You'll find out for sure someday."

Ed continued, "So, what got you into this war, Smitty?"

"The short version: I studied writing in college and thought I could get ideas for a book."

Ed told me he and Tucky would be my best bet because they both lasted the longest in their company.

"What about you, Lee? Where are you from, and what brings you to this war?"

"I'm from Virginia and -"

Ed interrupted, saying, "We have ourselves a *Johnny Reb*!"

Lee said, "Look, I'm no Reb, but my grandfather was. He fought with Robert E. Lee at Gettysburg. When he returned to watch them light *The Peace Flame Memorial*, he said men from both sides were there. He met other Rebs and even some Yanks. They both understood the terrors of the war and apologized for possibly wounding any of them or their friends. They doled out forgiveness and shared their sorrow over a few cold beers and many tears. After that trip, he shared some stories of the Civil War we had never heard. A couple of weeks afterward, he died. My mother told me before that trip she never saw him so happy."

Ed told him, "That's a good story; maybe Smitty can use it in his book. I thought it over; you're not Johnny Reb. You're just Reb. Now, if you two don't mind, I'm going out for a smoke. Are you joining me, Tucky?"

"No, I better stay here and get these men settled," Tucky replied.

Lee said, offended, "Where does he get off calling me Reb? He seems like nothing but trouble. I don't see why they let guys like him in the army."

Tucky answered, "You got Ed all wrong. You'll never hear anyone say anything bad about him. He saved my life in North Africa. You'll meet a couple of other men whose lives he saved. He likes to give nicknames to everyone."

Reb asked, "If Ed's so great, why is he only a private?"

Tucky said, "He always turns down promotions."

"No one turns down a promotion. Tell me why." Tucky told us Ed made a promise to his mother.

"What promise?" asked Reb.

Then Tucky told us he would explain, but only if we could keep a secret. See, Tucky told Ed that he would never repeat the story but said we might only understand Ed with it. We promised him the secret was safe with us.

Tucky started by saying that he and Ed met at boot camp. While there, Ed got letters from his mother and his girl-friend, Betty. "I wasn't getting any mail, so I asked him if I could read some of his. He agreed but, of course, wouldn't let me read Betty's. We later discovered that I wasn't getting any letters because another Kenneth Tuck was in the company.

One day I read a letter from his mother, at the bottom she had written 'Don't forget your promise to me.' I asked him what the promise was. He told me he spoke with his parents the night before leaving for boot camp.

His mother said, "I want you to promise me that you won't make a decision that causes anyone to get killed."

Ed told her, "I'm not very educated, mother. They won't put me in charge of anyone."

Ed's father turned to his mother and said, "Let me talk to Ed. He can give you his answer in the morning."

After Ed's mother went upstairs, his father said, "Do you remember your mother's brother, Uncle John?" Ed nodded. His father continued, "When they lived down east, he worked in a coal mine for about seven years - not as a boss or a foreman. He was just a regular miner. One day, an explosion occurred while your uncle and five men were in the mine. He helped three other men to safety, but two men died. One of the men who died was the brother of your mother's best friend, Sally. At the funeral, Sally told your mother that she would never speak to her again or forgive your Uncle John as long as she lived. About a month later, your mother moved to Brockway with her father and your Uncle John. That is why she is asking you to make her this promise."

Ed asked, "What should I tell her?"

His father told him, "You have until morning to come up with your answer."

Ed told me he didn't sleep a wink. When his parents took him to the train depot, his mother asked if he had considered her request. He explained he would agree to the promise if she also promised him something. "If any of my brothers get into this war, don't make them promise you the same thing."

She agreed, kissed and hugged him, and whispered in his ear: "Remember, a promise is forever."

Tucky continued, "You see, Ed's not troublesome; he's a hell of a soldier." Just then, a new soldier entered the barracks and asked, "Who's a hell of a good soldier?"

Tucky answered, "Ed Hrinya, and who are you?"

"My name is Donald Francis Olson, Jr. Most everyone calls me Junior."

Tucky said, "Junior? You look more like a freshman."

"I'm 18 years old, just graduated high school."

Tucky said, "You two help Junior get settled in. I'm going to find Ed." Then he left.

Junior said, "Just once, I wish someone would welcome me instead of making fun of me."

Meanwhile, Tucky found Ed and told him he got us settled in. He also said, "Another soldier arrived. You should see him; he said his name was Donald Francis Olson Jr. I told him he looked like a freshman. I can hardly wait to introduce you to him." Ed put out his cigarette and followed Tucky. When they got to the barracks, Junior had his back turned to them. Tucky said, "Junior, I want you to meet Ed Hrinya."

Junior turned around. Ed turned pale and paused for a few seconds before saying, "Welcome to England, soldier. Let me know if there's anything I can do for you," Then he exited the room as quickly as he had entered.

Tucky followed him, asking, "What was that? I was sure you were going to pick on Junior."

Ed said, "Don't you know who that soldier is?"

Tucky answered, "Donald Francis Olson, Jr."

Ed becoming more frantic, yelled, "That's not who that is!"

"Then tell me who it is, Ed!"

"It's my little brother!" Ed continued, "When he turned around, Tucky, I... thought...I... well, I thought I was staring at my little brother. I already have two brothers in this war, and he will be involved if this war lasts much longer! If I can do anything to end this war soon, I'll do it!" Ed was screaming by now and had to take a moment to calm himself. "Do me a favor, and don't tell anyone about this," Ed said to Tucky.

After the last of our company arrived, we began our basic training in England. We marched, studied maps, and learned to fire our rifles there. I had a chance to get to know some of the men. Junior was from Texas and had three younger brothers. Reb lived on a farm his family had owned for generations. Tucky was married to his high school sweetheart and, until his time in the army, had never left his small town in Iowa. I tried to get Ed to tell me some things about himself, but he wasn't quick to open up.

Ed was more interested in learning about me. He asked

what my father did. I told him he had been a police officer for twenty years. "What kind of cop was he," asked Ed.

"A local cop," I told him.

Ed said, "That's not what I mean. Was he a good cop or a bad cop?" He continued before I could answer him, "I remember Chief Jackson back in Brockway. He was one of the good ones. One night he tried to break up a fight and was shot. Just like that, his life was over. After he died, his widow took their children and moved back to Ohio to live with her parents. Even though I was young, I'll never forget learning from him to make the best of every moment."

I nodded solemnly and told Ed, "My father left the police force, and now he drives a taxi in Gettysburg. He doesn't make as much money, but my mother sleeps better at night."

I told Ed that even though I had never heard of Brockway, it couldn't be too bad based on how he spoke about it. "Did anyone famous come from Brockway," I asked. Ed replied, "No one yet, but my friend Smokey Joe Himes will change that. Smokey Joe was a baseball pitcher. He was outstanding back in school. Scouts from as far away as St. Louis came to Brockway to see him pitch. He's in the Navy now, serving in the Pacific. If it weren't for this war, he might be in the pros by now."

As the day of Operation Overlord drew closer, our training became more intense. One night Captain Johnson and Sergeant McCall were in our barracks going over the plan. He told us we had to take out a machine-gun battery and that the lives of many men depended on us. When they finished, they asked if we had any questions.

Junior asked if they could explain about non-combative

soldiers. Captain Johnson said that there are rules in wars. "One of those rules is you're not to shoot at a non-combative, but you are combative soldiers. You are to try to make it across the beach safely. You can't go backward, even if it's to save Sergeant McCall or me." When there were no more questions, he said, "Lights out in ten minutes."

Ed could tell Junior was nervous and asked him about it. Junior said he had a recurring nightmare of getting killed on the day of the invasion. Ed assured him he would watch out for him and ensure he was safe. "I promise to keep you safe, and a promise is forever."

"Thanks, Ed," said Junior, "I appreciate that."

2

The Chicken Coup

Ed noticed another soldier, Joe Collins, or "Big Joe," as we called him, looking sad. Ed asked him, "What is wrong?"

Big Joe said, "My birthday is in a few days, and this will be the third in a row away from home," he added, "my mother used to make me my favorite meal."

Ed asked him, "What was that?"

He answered, "Fried chicken."

Ed told him, "Let me. I'll take care of that for you." smirked Ed.

Ed turned to Reb then and asked, "Do your friends still work in the mess tent?"

He said, "Yes."

Big Joe interrupted, "You don't understand, Ed. The best fried chicken comes from freshly killed chickens. My mother would go to a farm, and the farmer would kill the chickens and prepare them for her to fry."

Ed told him, "I have worked on a farm, and I'll be able to handle that."

Junior asked, "Where will you get the chickens?" Ed told him, "Every day when we use the train, we pass by farms. There have to be chickens on one of them."

Junior asked, "Are you going to ask Captain Johnson if we can stop and get some chickens? "

"He'd never let us do that."

Tucky asked, "Then how do you plan on getting chickens?"

Ed told him with a sly grin, "We'll break out and steal them, of course!"

"Who is this 'we' you are referring to?" asked Tucky. Ed replied, "I think I'm looking right at them."

"Why me?!" Tucky relented.

"I saved your life - Junior, you're going, too."

"Why me," asked Junior.

"Because I promised to watch out for you." He turned to me and said, "Smitty, you're coming, too."

"Why me? You never saved my life, and you never promised to watch out for me." I asked him.

Ed explained, "You want to be a writer, don't you? This story will be one for the books!"

I reasoned with him, "What if we break out and get to a farm? How do you plan on stealing those chickens?"

Ed replied, "Didn't I ever tell you I was a chicken thief?"

"Okay...but what if you can't devise a plan to pull this off?"

"If I can't, we'll call it off, but I have a few days to work on it."

A few days later, Ed went over the plan with us. All of us would scout the best chicken farm from the train. Then we would vote on which made for the easiest job. The night we were to break out, men from our barracks would volunteer to watch guard. We had to get back before they were relieved to avoid explaining ourselves to someone unfamiliar with the plan. Once we got out of the camp, Ed would take the lead, grabbing the chickens and breaking their necks. We would carry the chickens back in bags we brought along, and the only thing left to account for would be enjoying the fried chicken. It seemed like a good enough plan.

Things went well for us until we were just about to leave. The farmer heard the commotion and, thinking it was a wild animal, came around the barn firing blind in the dark right at us. We ran as fast as we could until the farmer gave up his chase. As we slowed down to catch our breath, Ed was laughing and said, "I never saw you guys run so fast." I reminded him that a gun at our backs was as good an excuse as any to run.

We were discouraged when we returned to camp to see that the guards had changed early. Tucky said, "What do we do now?" You could tell by Ed's face that he was already formulating a plan.

Tucky blurted out in a whispered scream, "This better be good, or we may face the firing squad."

"Don't worry, and it'll work," said Ed.

We planned to enter at the opposite side of our station, avoiding the guards. Then, we were going to toss the chicken bags over the wire and crawl under the fence. When we gathered the bags, we would hide behind a barrack until we made it. Tucky planned to go first, then me, Junior, and finally Ed. Ed said, "If anything goes wrong, keep your mouth shut. Don't say a word. I'll talk for you."

Tucky and I made it through without a hitch. However, when Junior was about 5 feet from the barrack, a guard yelled, "Stop! Who's there?"

Junior froze in silence. The guard approached him and said, "What are you doing, private?" He remained silent. "Aren't you going to answer?" the guard asked.

Ed said, "I ordered him not to speak."

The guard asked, "Then maybe you can tell me what's going on, private."

Ed replied, "Private? I'm not a private. I'm a captain especially selected and trained for this assignment by General Patton."

"What assignment?"

"We're checking on the security of camps all across England."

"If you're a captain, why are you wearing a private's uniform?"

Ed told him, "Because if I wore my captain's uniform, you would let me pass without question." The guard said, "I think I better contact my officer."

Ed told him, "You will do no such thing unless you want to be court-martialed." The guard insisted that he should tell someone. Ed explained that while he and Junior got caught, two other soldiers behind the barrack came in unseen. "What were you doing, sleeping on duty?"

The guard said he'd let them go if he answered one question. "What's in the bags?" Ed told him, "Dead chickens."

"Dead chickens? Sirs?"

Ed continued, "General Patton and General Eisenhower both like fried chicken. So, they made a bet. Patton would get the chickens if we made it safely in here tonight. If we were caught, General Eisenhower would. It looks like Ike wins." Ed told him, "One last thing, private, no one is to know about this."

We gathered up our bags, and we went back to our barracks.

The next night, every soldier in our barracks had fried chicken. Ed retold the story of our nighttime adventure. All of a sudden, Captain Johnson and Sergeant McCall entered. The captain asked, "What is going on?"

Ed told him, "We were having fried chicken for Private Collins' birthday. Didn't Private Tuck tell you? He was supposed to invite you. We have plenty. Do you want some?" The captain commented, "I haven't had fried chicken in years." So, they both joined us. The captain led us in singing "Happy Birthday." It was one of the bright spots for those men in an awful war.

The next day I had several minutes alone with Ed. I asked him how he was so brave.

"Why do you ask?"

I told him, "When the farmer was shooting at us, it didn't seem to bother you."

He told me, "I knew something you didn't. The farmer wasn't trying to hit us." I asked him, "How can you be so sure?"

He said, "Remember when I told you I was a chicken thief?" He continued, "When I was a sophomore in school, I dropped out and got a job working for farmer Strishock. He wouldn't pay me cash. He would give my parents milk, butter, eggs, and from time to time, money. I had worked there a few years when the McKay brothers, Norman and Howard, asked me if I would like to join them in stealing chickens. Every couple of weeks, we'd hit a different farm. One day they told me we were going to hit Strishock's place. I told them I didn't want to do it because he had been good to us. But they convinced me if we didn't hit his place, people might get suspicious of me.

"So, we did, and things went well until we started to leave. Old Man Strishock came around his barn, shooting his shotgun. We barely got away. From that day on, we vowed never to steal chickens again.

"A year later, I left Strishock's Farm for a job at the clay pipe plant. About two years later, he died. After the funeral, my dad saw me crying. He tried to console me, saying, "I know you liked Mr. Strishock a lot."

I told him, "It wasn't just that there was something I meant to tell him, but I never had the chance."

My dad asked, "What did you want to tell him?"

I told him, "I wanted to let Mr. Strishock know that the McKay brothers and I were the ones who stole his chickens."

My dad told me, "He already knew that. "He overheard you boys at the back of the hardware store. He came and told your mother and me. We were going to talk to you about it, but he said he had a plan. He told us that you were the best worker he ever had and didn't want to lose you. So he planned to hide behind his barn, jump out, and fire in the air to scare you and your friends. He figured it would scare you enough that you would stop stealing chickens. After that night, word got around that farmers were going to shoot, so it prevented others from trying what you boys did. Mr. Strishock held back some money every month until he recouped his losses."

"Now you see, Smitty, why I wasn't scared. That farmer just wanted to scare us and let other soldiers know that they won't be as lucky as us. He'll ask the army for his money, and they'll give it to him."

"Jimmer," Smitty continued, "Ed was quite a soldier. He always shared what he knew about being a good soldier: how to march properly, clean your rifle, and shine your boots. I can't remember a time in England when his uniform wasn't spotless."

3

Operation Overlord

Normandy France, June 6, 1944

Shortly after the chicken incident, our training ended. We loaded into a landing craft and headed to the beach. As we got closer to the coast, one of the lookout men up front couldn't see anything due to the smoke. Captain Johnson must have seen the worry on my face. He tapped me on the shoulder, saying, "You don't have to worry, son. Our assignment is a piece of cake. Speaking of cake," he said, "we never had a piece of cake with those stolen chickens. We will have one together when this operation is over."

Mere minutes later, the landing gear went down, and the scene around us played out in fast-forward as we rushed towards the beach. To this day, I still don't know how I safely made it to our rallying point. Ed, Tucky, and a few other men were there when I got there. A couple more arrived, and one said he saw a grenade hit Captain Johnson and kill him. As I looked back, I saw Sergeant McCall get struck in the throat, I tried to go back to help him, but Ed stopped me. Ed asked, "Has anyone seen Junior?" No one had.

Above all the noise and commotion, we heard a faint voice crying: "Help me! Please help me! Please, somebody, help me!" It was Reb.

Ed darted towards him while Tucky yelled, "Get back here!" Ed caught up to Reb, who got caught on a barrier.

Reb was a crying mess begging Ed to get him the hell out of there and take him home. "Tell them to quit shooting at me," Reb said, "and radio for the boats to come and get us."

Ed told him, "We have to get across the beach - your friend Smitty is up there, and so is Tucky."

Reb asked, "What about Junior?"

Ed told him, "He isn't there yet, but he will be soon. Follow me, and you'll be safe."

They crossed the beach under heavy fire but arrived safely. Tucky yelled at Ed, "What were you thinking? You could have died!"

"Shut up, Tucky. Just shut up," Ed said.

Tucky asked, "What do we do now?"

Ed yelled, "We can't stay here, or we'll get killed."

More men continued to trickle into our rallying point. One of them asked if we were with Dog Company. Tucky told him we were Fox Company. He said, "If you're Fox's, where's Dog?"

Tucky pointed and said, "Probably in that direction."

The soldier explained, "They taught us in training to fall

in with the first company we found if we got separated from ours. Who's in charge here?"

Tucky said, "What?"

"Who's the highest-ranking soldier in this section of the beach?"

Tucky paused a second and pointed to Ed. The soldier said, "He's just a private."

Tucky told him, "You got it wrong. He's a captain especially selected and trained for this assignment by General Patton. Isn't that right, captain?"

Ed could see the fear in our eyes. "That's right private. Our orders are to proceed down this beach, follow the gully and take out the machine gun battery. If we all make it, or just one of us, we must achieve our objective."

Ed ordered Reb and me to lead the assault. The rest of our company followed. Dog Company's men would fall behind Fox, with Tucky and Ed trailing at the back. Sometimes the gunfire was so close we could hear the bullets whipping past us. The sand was flying through the smoke-filled air, and we slowly edged our way to the guns and detonated them with the last of our grenades. We met our objective with only a few more injuries. There were several wounded soldiers, and my upper arm was bleeding.

Ed commanded us to secure the area against a counter-attack while he had the radio operator send out the message that our sector was open. He sent me to the medic to check my arm.

Later in the day, a captain from Dog Company arrived. He asked one of his soldiers who was in charge. The soldier pointed to Ed. The captain approached Ed and asked, "Are you in charge, captain?"

Tucky interrupted, "I can explain, sir. Ed is a private, and we knew our captain and sergeant had died. Some men from Dog Company fell in with us. I told them Ed was our captain because the men and I trusted him. He gave us our orders, and our mission was a success." The captain asked Ed, "Is that true?"

"It is," he answered.

The captain said, "I'm sure there will be a promotion for you."

Ed retorted, "I don't deserve a promotion."

The captain asked, "Why do you say that?"

"We had been trained to accomplish our objective. How I see it, we were following orders." Ed added, "if there's anyone who should receive a promotion, it's Private Smith and Lee. They led the assault, and Private Smith was wounded." The captain told us he would take over and told us to get something to eat.

Ed said, "Captain, a soldier was with us. His name was Donald Francis Olson, Jr., from Texas. We don't know what happened to him."

The captain informed us that the army was already gathering the list of casualties and would pass it on to us when it was complete.

Ed and Tucky went together to eat. Tucky said, "You were good today, Ed."

Ed replied, "Don't ever yell at me like that again, Tucky. You know about the promise I made to my mother to keep these men alive at all costs. I had to save Reb, and now I'm worried about Junior."

Tucky assured him, "Don't worry about Junior. Remember how he was always going in the wrong direction during our training? He probably fell in with a different company."

Reb and I spoke to the captain, and then we joined Tucky and Ed. Reb told Ed, "The captain told us you deserved a promotion, and what you said about Smitty and me. I don't deserve a promotion. I was a coward."

Ed told him, "Being scared doesn't make you a coward. Hell, if that were the case, we were all cowards!"

Reb told him, "You weren't. You saved my life."

"Don't think for one second that I wasn't scared down there today. If you were a coward, you would have told the soldier who asked who was in charge that we should wait for an officer or even a corporal to give us orders. You followed my orders, led the assault, and were an integral part of the success of this mission." And then Ed repeated, "You're not a coward." Ed repeated.

"From now on, I'm your go-to guy. I'll take care of anything you want. Just ask." Reb told Ed.

"What do you have to give me? I'll tell you what, if we both make it through this war, promise me you owe me one favor that I can cash in at any time." Reb promised. Ed reminded him that a promise is forever.

About a week later, the captain sent a corporal around with a list of casualties. He asked Tucky where Ed was so that he could show it to him. Tucky told him, "I'll look over the list and tell Ed what's on it." Tucky read under his breath, "Captain Johnson, Sergeant McCall, Big Joe..." Several others from our company were listed. More men were missing in action. He finally saw Junior's name. Next to it was written, "Wounded; sent back to England." Tucky asked the corporal where Junior would go after he recovered. The captain told him he would be sent back to the States with an honorable discharge. The corporal asked, "Have you seen everything that you need to?" Tucky told him, "I have," and went to find Ed.

Ed ran up to Tucky with anticipation saying, "The captain told me a corporal had the list I was waiting to see." Tucky told Ed about the list and what happened to Junior. "That's good news, and Ed," Tucky told him, "you kept your promise to your mother."

Ed's face relaxed into a sigh of relief. He told Tucky, "Remind me not to make another promise again!"

That night Tucky pulled me aside and said he needed to get something off his chest. He asked me to keep it between us. I told him I would. He said, "Junior spelled his last name O-l-s-o-n, with an O, right?"

"That's correct," I told him.

" The soldier on the list was Donald Francis O-l-s-E-n," he told me. "Don't let Ed know. It will just make him worry."

The war slowly progressed as we advanced across France. In October, we had a three-day pass in Paris. On the first night, we were in a bar. Tucky, Reb, Ed, and I were drinking when a soldier approached us and asked if we had heard the good news. "What good news?" we all said in unison. He told us that he had a brother on Ike's staff who overheard him say the war would be over by Christmas. We thanked him for the news.

I said, "What do you think about that, Ed?"

He said, "I'll only believe it when I hear it from Ike directly."

I turned to Reb, "Tell these guys about the reunion we're planning."

Reb told Tucky and Ed, "I have been gathering the names of everyone we served with since we got to England. Twenty-five years after the war ends, we'll all gather in Gettysburg. I asked Tucky if he'd come. Tucky told me he'd be there if Ed comes." Reb turned to Ed and asked, "What about it, Ed?"

"I'll be there if you invite Junior," Ed told him.

"As I said, I'm keeping track of everyone."

Tucky reiterated, "If that's the case, I promise to be there too."

While talking and drinking, another soldier approached our table and asked if any of us were from Pennsylvania. Perplexed and a little drunk, I told him both Ed and I were from there. He said a soldier gave him two dollars to find someone from Pennsylvania because he'd never met anyone from there that he couldn't beat up. I asked how big the soldier who wanted to fight us was. He wouldn't tell us, saying, "I only got paid to deliver a man from Pennsylvania."

We sat there about a minute before Tucky asked, "What are you going to do?"

Ed told him, "I'm going to finish my beer."

Reb wondered out loud, "Are you afraid?"

"I'm not afraid," Ed said with a smirk, "I'll let Smitty fight him if I think I can't handle it."

We went outside and looked around, but no one was there. Tucky said, "I wonder where that soldier is?" A voice came behind us in a mock-deep voice, saying, "I'm here." We turned around and were surprised to find Junior! We all thought someone had slipped a hallucinogen into our drinks and asked him what the hell he was doing there. He told us he was there on the last day of a pass. We wanted to know what had happened to him during the landing. He explained he got separated from us and fell in with another company. "I tried to get back with you, but they ordered me to stay."

Ed said, "We got a list saying you were wounded and heading back to the States."

Junior said, "That wasn't me."

I noticed an extra stripe on his shoulder and said, "We'll have to call you Corporal Olson from now on."

He said, "I owe this stripe to you, Ed. When I first got to England, Tucky told me you were a hell of a soldier. I tried to follow your example and prove myself worthy of a promotion when the time came."

We invited him to join us, but he told us he had to return to camp. They were pulling out in the morning. I told Reb to tell him about the reunion. Junior said, "That is a great idea." He added, "If anything should happen to me between now and then, ya'll raise a glass and toast a hell of a good soldier, Junior Olson."

To the surprise of a few, the war was not over by Christmas. We fought in the Bulge, and the war edged close to being won for our allies by springtime. They stationed us in a nearby village for about a month. We received orders to move out to another town ten miles away.

Local nuns ran an orphanage in that village. Ed told all the soldiers to gather their extra candy bars and gum for the children. Before we left, Ed gave them to the nuns and asked them if they needed anything else. One of the nuns told him that most of their musical instruments were stolen or destroyed. She asked, "If you come across a piano somewhere, we would appreciate it if you brought it back to us."

Ed promised her, "If we find one, we'll bring it back here."

Tucky elbowed Ed reminding him, "You aren't supposed to make any promises."

Our captain ordered us to spread out and search the city when we arrived in the next town. Reb and I went down one side of the street while Tucky and Ed searched the other. Ed said to Tucky, "Look in there," Tucky peered into the window and saw a piano. Ed said, "There's our piano!"

After searching the town, we reported that everything was secure.

Ed told the captain about the piano and said he wanted to give it to the nuns. The captain asked him, "Why do you want to do that?"

Ed told him, "If we could accomplish something good out of all the bad we've seen in this war, then some small parts would be worth it." Ed added, "I promised the nuns, and a promise is forever."

We got a soldier to bring the tank to the building where the piano was and secured it to the back. Ed turned to us and said, "Tucky, you and Smitty are going."

Reb asked, "Why can't I go?"

Ed told him, "Tucky and I have been together since boot camp," he added, "I'm taking Smitty because he's writing a book." Before we left, Reb asked me to be careful.

We slowly walked behind the tank, ensuring the piano

didn't fall off. The nuns were surprised to see us so soon and impressed that Ed kept his promise. We spent the night but left at first light. On the way back, we rode on the tank. I asked Ed about the nickname General Patton gave him. I said, "Is it true that he's the only one you let call you that?"

Ed told me, "That's true," he added, "I'll let Tucky tell you the story."

"You don't mind, Ed?" asked Tucky.

"No, I don't since I told you the truth," Ed said.

Tucky began by saying, "Way back in basic training, Ed told everyone he was friends with General Patton. He probably thought we would never meet him. We were at a staging area helping the British defeat Rommel in North Africa. Patton happened to be there. The men of our unit said since they were friends and all that, Ed should go over and ask him to inspect the troops. Ed told them, as a matter of fact, he would. As he left, I yelled, "If he's your friend, hitch a ride in his Jeep!" Ed went to the general and congratulated him on leading a successful campaign. The general thanked him, so Ed asked if he would like to inspect the troops. The general replied, "This seems like an odd request from a private, but I don't see why not." Ed, stretching his good luck further, requested the privilege of riding in his Jeep. Patton asked, "Why should I let you ride with me?" Ed spilled to the general that it was because he told the men he was his friend and needed to prove it by riding in his Jeep. Patton asked Ed if they had ever met. Ed admitted they had not. The general said, "You're a pest - Rommel was a pest, but at least he was a general. They call him 'The Desert Fox.' I'm going to call you 'The Desert Flea.' With that, they rode over together in his Jeep, and the general did inspect the troops just as he said. When he finished, one of our men asked him if he knew Private Hrinya before today. With a puzzled expression, Patton said, "Is that what you all call him? I call him 'The Desert Flea,' but I'm the only one who can call him that." Ed told me the truth about him and Patton but asked that I keep it between us. I have because I always do what Ed tells me."

As Tucky finished his story, Ed must have noticed the tank ride was getting bumpy. He turned to me and said, "Tucky and I have ridden on tanks before, so listen when I tell you to be careful. A tank is like a bucking bronco."

Almost on cue, the tank hit a ditch and tossed me to the ground just in front of it. Ed jumped off and rolled me out of its way just before it would have crushed me. Tucky yelled at the tank driver to stop.

I was still shaking and told Ed, "You saved another life today." He told me it was nothing, but I persisted, saying, "I'm going to find a way to make it up to you."

Ed said, "Following the war, you can." I promised him I would.

We jumped back into the tank and continued back to our comrades. As we approached the town, we heard bells ringing and gunfire. Ed sensed something was wrong and told us to get our rifles ready. Just then, we saw Reb running towards us. He screamed at us, "Have you heard the news?! "The war is over - Ike announced it not long ago!" We were unable to contain our excitement. For a soldier, the happiest day of his life is when the shooting ceases.

4

News of Corporal Olson

Following the war, the army began to discharge soldiers methodically. A month later, our company arrived at the transfer station. Ed and Tucky were leaving the next day. Reb gathered all the soldier's information for the reunion. Tucky told him, "You have 25 years to get ready." Reb told him he wanted to write to keep in touch.

A soldier stopped as he was passing by and said, "Ed? Ed Hrinya from Brockway, Pennsylvania?"

Ed jumped to his feet and embraced him. "Bob Hetrick, is that you?"

"It's me," Bob replied. "How have you been, Ed?"

"Good, now that the war is over! Fellows, this is Bob Hetrick. He's from Brockway, Pennsylvania."

"Did you hear about your friend Smokey Joe Himes?" Bob asked. "He was killed when the ship he was serving in sunk. Most of the men in his company were lost. I'm sorry, Ed, but it was sure good to see you! Do you know when you're going home?" Ed told him tomorrow.

Another soldier came up to us and asked, "Do you know where I could find a soldier named Ed Hrinya from Brockway, Pennsylvania?"

Ed said, "I'm him."

The soldier explained, "I've been looking for you for some time. I came here to deliver a letter from Corporal Donald Francis Olson, Jr."

Ed told him, "I'm glad you found me today. I'm leaving for home tomorrow. How is Junior?"

"He said you'd call him that."

"Where is he now," Ed inquired, "probably already on his way home to Texas, and -..." ---

"I'm sorry to tell you, he got killed in the line of duty," the soldier interrupted. "But he told me to find you even if that meant going to Brockway to deliver this letter and tell you what happened."

The soldier continued, "The corporal and five of us were on patrol when we saw a man waving a white flag. When we seized him, he begged us to go to his village a few miles away. He told us there were German citizens ready to surrender and that the townspeople had food to share, so we followed him.

"When we arrived, the Germans weren't ready to concede after all. They asked us the name of the town where we were staying. When we told them, they responded that they had heard rumors the people hid all of their valuables in the church's basement. We told them we checked everything twice, and barely anything was left - only the elderly and orphans remained.

"They didn't believe us and started threatening to kill civilians if we didn't bring them the valuables. The German soldier turned to our captain and shot him point blank. I got away and returned to the village where Corporal Olson was. The corporal gathered weapons and said we were returning to help save the town. I told the corporal that wasn't our order, but he mentioned you, Ed. He said you told him we might win this war if we were all willing to sacrifice.

"When we arrived at the village, they had already killed seven men. Corporal Olson had more men and weapons, so he cut a deal with the German soldiers that we would not give chase if they left immediately. So, they went.

"As Corporal Olson gave us orders to organize a burial detail for the dead, a German soldier who stayed behind fired one shot. The bullet struck the corporal in the back. We returned fire and killed him. We ran over to confirm our kill and noticed he had shot the gun with his final round.

"The rest of the men tended to the corporal. When we returned, he asked us to get the children off the street because they had seen enough death. He knew his wound was fatal and asked me to visit his parents and tell them what had happened. He also wanted me to find you and tell you the same. He gave me the letter I gave to you. I promised him anything he asked and held his hand while he lay dying. We buried him in the village with a makeshift grave marker so anyone could visit. The people there said they would never forget what he did for them."

After the soldier finished telling Ed the story, he handed him Junior's letter and left. Ed opened the letter tearfully. Tucky said in a low voice, "Read it to us, Ed."

Ed began, *"Ed, I have respected you from the day I met you because you showed me respect when everyone else saw a kid. You are the only reason I am a corporal. You showed me how to be a good soldier. No matter what happens, I will always consider us friends. See you at the reunion. Junior."*

Ed broke down crying. "Damn it," he said.

Reb pulled out his notebook and began to write. Ed asked him, "What are you doing?"

He told him, "I'm recording about Junior in my reunion book." Ed felt the anger growing.

He spewed at Reb, "Is that all Junior was to you? Just, just... another soldier coming to your reunion? Just another numbered seat?! If that's all he is, I won't be there! Remember when I saved your life? You promised me after the war, I could ask you for anything! So here it is; I want you to give me your word that you won't write to me, especially about your stupid reunion!"

Tucky intervened, "Don't get mad at Reb, Ed. We are all sad about Junior."

Ed became inconsolable. "I broke... the promise... to my mother."

Tucky replied, "She'll never hold Junior's death against you."

I jumped in and said, "Tucky told us about the promise you made, and he's right. Your mother won't hold you responsible."

Ed's sadness turned to anger after that. "Tucky, who all did you tell," he asked.

Tucky told him, "Just Reb and Smitty."

Ed said, "you told me you would never tell that story. I never want to talk to you again. Not today, not tomorrow, not on the ship back to the States. Not ever!" He turned to me, almost snarling now, and said, "As for you, Smitty, I saved your life, and now I want your word that you'll never write that book, even if you change names. You're not allowed to write that book!" Then he stormed off.

The next day Tucky said his goodbyes to Reb and me, but Ed left without saying a word. After I made it back home to the States, I contacted Tucky. He told me Ed was true to his word, and he had not heard from him once. I sent letters to Ed for over a year before I decided he truly wanted to be left alone.

5

Life After the War

"Reb and I became close friends throughout the war, and our friendship remained that way after we returned home. I was his best man when he married in '46. He returned the favor when I married in 1949. I finished my education and became an English teacher at a local school in Gettysburg. Reb bought a farm in Virginia. When he had children, our kids were like brothers and sisters. Growing up, they spent summer vacations together. We both stayed busy with our careers and families. Reb spent most of his free time in close contact with the soldiers in our company, keeping up with their lives and planning the reunion.

"Sadly, in 1967, Reb was killed in an automobile accident. After his passing, Reb's widow recruited my wife and me to help her with the reunion. We immediately sent out letters informing everyone about Reb. Of course, I sent one to

Ed. Many of the men sent their sympathies, but Ed never responded.

"In the fall of 1969, I sent out reunion invitations. We were going to hold it on July 3-5, 1970, in Gettysburg. To my surprise, Betty answered for Ed, saying they would not attend.

6

The Reunion

"In the spring of 1970, I sent out one last reminder asking everyone to RSVP. I didn't think it would hurt, so I sent one to Ed. We planned to hold the reunion from Friday evening till Sunday after lunch. We would have a social time Friday night and tour the battlefield on Saturday. Then Saturday night, we planned to have a banquet and memorial service for all who passed away. After Sunday lunch, we would depart for home.

"The day of the reunion came at last. Reb's widow, my wife, and I were helping people register and handing out name tags to everyone as they arrived. I looked down the hallway and saw someone I hadn't seen in a quarter-century. I excused myself and walked down the hallway."

"Ed, is that you?" I asked.

He smiled solemnly and said, "Smitty, it's nice to see you.

Is there someplace we can go? I want to talk." I told him to wait there and walked back up the hallway. My wife instinctively knew it was Ed.

I told her, "He wants to talk alone. I'll be right back."

I returned to Ed, and we walked to my hotel room to speak privately. I said, "The last I heard from you, Betty said you two wouldn't be attending. Where is Betty, Ed?" He told me she died in March from a stroke. It was quick, and the doctors said most likely painless. He went on to say that he wanted to tell me about the past 25 years.

Ed began his story on his first day back. "When I returned to Brockway, my mother and father met me at the train station. My mother asked me almost immediately if I had kept the promise to her. I told her I had. She told me that her best friend visited about a year ago -the one who said she would never speak to her again. My mother told her friend about the promise between us. Her friend said she should have never placed that burden solely on my shoulders - not for her sake or her brother's. My parents told me I didn't have to discuss the war with them if I wanted to move on. My dad informed me that my two brothers had safely made it through the war and would be home around the same time as us."

His younger brother was waiting there when they returned to the house. He asked Ed if he had heard about Smokey Joe. Ed told him he had.

Ed's brother told him he and a bunch of the guys already went over to see if Joe's brothers wanted to play baseball. When they knocked at the door, his sister answered and told us they had just received the notice that he did not survive." His mother came to the door to greet them. Ed's brother told her, "I'm sorry to hear about Smokey Joe - I mean your son Joseph. We'll leave you in peace to grieve."

She said, "No, they should play ball today. That's what Joseph would want."

So, they played ball and shared stories about their fallen comrade. They remembered the day he told the best hitter from Brookville that he could strike him out blindfolded and proved it. Then another day, when the scout from St. Louis came, Joe threw a one-hitter and struck out twelve.

His little brother ended the story quickly, asking Ed, "How bad was it? The war, I mean?"

Ed told him, "Not bad where I was."

Ed looked me in the eyes and said he never talked about the war to anyone, not even his brothers.

He got his old job back at the clay pipe plant and married Betty. In 1946 Betty got pregnant with their first child. One day, while she was gardening in their front yard, a car pulled up, and someone asked her, "Does Ed Hrinya live here?" She said he did and called Ed outside.

"Ed, there's someone here to see you."

"Who is it, Betty?"

"I don't know," she replied. Ed came outside and saw a man, a woman, and three boys coming toward him. Betty whispered out of the side of her mouth, "Ed, who are they?" He answered, "I don't know."

The man extended his hand towards Ed. He said, "You must be Ed Hrinya."

"I am, and this is my wife, Betty," said Ed. The man continued his introductions, "This is my wife and our three sons.

I've wanted to meet you for a while now. I'm Donald Francis Olson Sr. Our son, Junior, was in the army with you."

Betty interjected, "Mrs. Olson, you and your boys can come inside, and I'll give you some lemonade. I think these men will probably want to speak to each other." They followed her inside.

Mr. Olson said, "From the time Junior met you, whenever he would write home, he mentioned you. He told us how you treated him as an equal and taught him how to be a good soldier. Last year a soldier came by and told us how Junior died. He mentioned that he told you the same story and gave you Junior's letter."

Ed told Mr. Olson, "a day doesn't go by that I don't think about Junior. I believe something I said may have cost him his life. He reminded me so much of my kid brother, and I couldn't protect him."

Mr. Olson put his arm on Ed's shoulder and said, "It's not your fault. What Junior and his men did saved lives. Back home in Texas, they dedicated a monument to those who died in the war from our town. On that monument are 23 names, along with Junior's. Many people sacrificed to free the world of that evil regime." Donald Sr. continued, "I recently got a job offer in Buffalo. We saw on the map that our trip would bring us through Brockway, so we decided to meet the man who left an impression on our son."

Betty, Mrs. Olson, and the boys came outside. Betty had made sandwiches for their trip, "We better be going," Mr. Olson said, "Once again, thank you for taking our son under your wing."

Ed told him, "You can't leave yet. You haven't introduced me to your sons."

Mr. Olson said, "You knew Junior. We named him after me, of course. Then pointing one at a time, he said, "This is Travis William, Bowie James, and Davy - named after Davy Crockett."

Ed started telling the boys about their brother but couldn't continue because he broke down crying.

Mr. Olson interrupted and said, "It's alright. We've got to get going."

Ed told me he turned to his wife right after the Olsons left and said, "Betty, if we have a son, I want to name him Donald Francis."

Ed continued, "Our first child was a daughter. We named her after my mother, Margaret Mary. Our second was a son. We named him Donald Francis, but everyone called him Junior. We had three more sons, Travis William, Bowie James, and Davey Edward. I received your letter a few years back telling me about Reb and how you were taking over the reunion. Last year when we got your letter, I told Betty to respond. This spring, shortly after she died, your invitation arrived. I came across it again last week. I told Margaret Mary I needed time alone and was going away for the weekend. I didn't tell her where I was going. I hope you don't mind me showing up, Smitty."

I told him, "I don't mind at all."

About 300 people attended the reunion between the men and their spouses or widows. I introduced Ed to Reb's widow, Rebecca. He greeted my wife, Evelyn. She said, "Smitty has told me so much about you."

I explained to him, "Tucky is sick and couldn't make the trip from Iowa."

On Friday night, Ed spent the evening renewing friendships and telling stories. Ed never mentioned how he saved Tucky's life in North Africa but explained how General Patton gave him the nickname 'The Desert Flea.' He told the story of the stolen chickens, but he never mentioned how scared we were when the farmer shot at us. He didn't speak about how fearless he seemed through it all. He talked about the D-Day invasion but not about saving Reb's life or taking charge after Captain Johnson's death. He did tell how Reb and I led the assault on the machine gun battery and how we got a piano for the nuns, but not how he saved my life.

Towards the end of Friday night, I told Ed I had someone I would like him to meet. I introduced him to Captain Johnson. He's the son of our Captain Johnson. "He graduated from West Point and is home from Vietnam."

Ed told him, "You should be proud of your father. He was a great leader."

I spent all day Saturday with Ed. After breakfast, we toured the battlefield. On Saturday evening, we held our banquet and memorial service. During the memorial service, I read many of the names of the men who were either killed in the war or had passed away since. When I got to Reb's, I told everyone the reunion was always Reb's idea. When I got to Junior's name, I let Ed do the honors. He said, "Donald Francis Olson Jr, or Junior as we called him. Raise your glasses and toast one hell of a soldier."

The men agreed that the reunion was a great idea. They wanted to get together every year. Different men volunteered to host the reunion at local venues, making it easier for more to attend. George Slattery from Louisville was selected to host the following year's reunion.

After lunch on Sunday, I told Ed, "There is something I want to show you." As we drove over, I asked him, "Do you plan on coming to next year's reunion?"

Ed answered, "I don't think so. I only attended this one because I promised Reb."

We arrived at the site I wanted to show him. I told Ed, "This is the site of the Peace Flame. The same one Reb's grandfather came here to see after the civil war. Reb and I made the trip back when they lit it in 1963 for the 100th anniversary of the battle. The moment we got here, Reb started crying."

"I suppose it was quite emotional for him," Ed said.

I told Ed, "It's not that. He cried because the man who saved his life didn't want to communicate with him. As it turned out, he never heard from you again."

Ed bowed his head and said, "I realize I was wrong to treat Reb that way."

I said to Ed, "I still have all my notes. I think I have a good story to tell."

Ed told me, "You promised not to write that book, and a promise is forever." He said, "You have my address," and he gave me his phone number and told me to stay in touch, "if anything changes, I'll let you know."

"I invited Ed to every one of the annual reunions, but he never attended another. My wife and I went every year. In 1974 Tucky passed, and I read his name at the memorial service. In '92, Rebecca passed away.

"In 1994, my wife and I planned to visit England and France for the 50th anniversary of D-Day. We asked Ed to join us, but he declined. He said he was surprised I would want to return there to all the awful memories. He did ask me to find the graves of the men we served with and say a prayer. When we returned, I called and told him we paid our respects to our fallen comrades. We sent him lots of photographs and a video that we had made.

"In 1995, I sent him an invitation to the reunion. Margaret Mary wrote to tell us he had passed away. She said her father never mentioned the reunions. I read Ed's name at the memorial service that year in Denver. When we returned home, my wife said I could write my book now that Ed had passed. I told her that I promised Ed that I wouldn't, and a promise is forever. Instead, we put all my notes in a safe and videotaped me telling the same story I'm telling you. When we both pass away, our kids get it all, with instructions to pass on the story to Ed's children.

"My wife passed away last December. My granddaughter is getting married in Ohio this weekend, and my daughter asked me to come out a few days early. When I planned the trip, I saw that Brockway wasn't far from the interstate, so I planned a stop to pay my respects. I stopped at the Legion hall and asked if anyone knew where Ed lay to rest. They directed me to this cemetery. The groundskeeper brought me over to his grave. That's when I broke down, and you came upon me.

Smitty placed his hand on the tombstone and whispered a thank you to Ed.

7

The Promise

Brockway, PA 2000

Smitty said, "That's my story, Jimmer. Do you think I'm right to hold Ed in such high regard?"

Jimmer replied, "Smitty, there's something I need to tell you."

Smitty interrupted him, saying, "Remember before I told you this story that I asked you to do me a favor? The favor is you can't repeat this story to anyone, not even Ed's kids. You promised, and a promise is forever. Now, what was it you wanted to tell me?"

Jimmer stumbled on his words and finally said, "I…I guess I forgot. Must not have been important."

The two men shook hands before walking back toward their cars. Jimmer told Smitty to have a safe trip and to enjoy his granddaughter's wedding. Smitty got in his car and pulled away.

As Jimmer was getting into his car, another vehicle pulled up. The driver put the window down and yelled, "Jimmer, what have you been doing? Your wife said you were coming here two hours ago."

"A man told me an interesting story," Jimmer yelled back.

The man in the vehicle asked, "What about?"

Jimmer says, "I'm not allowed to tell anyone."

The man says, "Not even your oldest brother?"

"Not even you, Donald Francis."

"Why did you call me that?"

Jimmer says, "That's your name."

His brother replied, "Yes, it is, but you already know everyone calls me Junior. Okay, Bowie James, let's get going. Your wife is waiting for you."

About the Author

Donald F. Hrinya is a local author. Born and raised in Brockway, Pennsylvania, with a pension for stories, country music, and giving back to the community.

9 7 9 8 9 8 7 3 5 1 6 2 8